Kayla
the Pottery Fairy

Special thanks to
Narinder Dhami

ORCHARD BOOKS
338 Euston Road, London NW1 3BH
Orchard Books Australia
Level 17/207 Kent Street, Sydney, NSW 2000
A Paperback Original

First published in 2014 by Orchard Books

HiT entertainment

A CIP catalogue record for this book is available
from the British Library.

ISBN 978 1 40833 141 5

3 5 7 9 10 8 6 4 2

Printed in Great Britain

The paper and board used in this paperback are natural recyclable
products made from wood grown in sustainable forests. The
manufacturing processes conform to the environmental regulations
of the country of origin.

Orchard Books is a division of Hachette Children's Books,
an Hachette UK company

www.hachette.co.uk

Kayla
the Pottery
Fairy

by Daisy Meadows

ORCHARD

www.rainbowmagic.co.uk

The Fairyland Palace

Sara Sketchley's house

Bridge

Rainspell

Island

Maze

Park

Carys's Jewellery Shop

Beach and Promenade

Jack Frost's
Ice Castle

Campsite

Girls' tent

Market Square

Mimosa Cottage

Pottery Hall

Sunshine Cake Shoppe

Polly Painterly's Workshop

Jack Frost's Spell

I'm a wonderful painter, you must have heard of me,
Marvel at my amazing artistic ability!
With palette, brush and paints in hand,
I'll be the most famous artist in the land!

The Magical Crafts Fairies can't stop me,
I'll steal their magic and then you'll see
That everyone, whatever the cost,
Will want a painting by Jack Frost!

Contents

Crafts Week 9

Art Attack! 23

Clay Catastrophe 37

In a Spin! 49

Precious Pot 57

Glittering Glazes 67

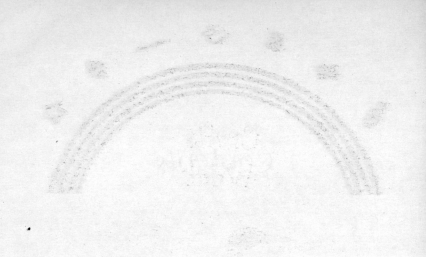

Crafts Week

"I can see Rainspell Island!" Rachel cried as the ferry sailed across the blue-green sea, foamy waves slapping against its sides. Ahead of them was a rocky island with soaring cliffs and crescents of golden sandy beaches around the coast. "Not far now, Kirsty."

"Aren't we lucky, Rachel?" Kirsty said, her face alight with excitement. "We came here not long ago for the music festival, and now we're back again for Crafts Week!"

"And maybe some fairy adventures, too?" Rachel murmured hopefully.

"Maybe, if we're *really* lucky," said Kirsty.

The girls had met for the first time when their families had both holidayed on Rainspell Island, and whilst exploring the island together, they'd made an amazing discovery. They'd found a tiny fairy called Ruby, and ever since then, Rachel and Kirsty had been loyal friends of the fairies. The girls had offered to help their magical friends many times when selfish Jack Frost and his naughty goblins were causing chaos in Fairyland.

The ferry docked at the jetty, and the girls' parents came up from below deck with all the luggage.

"That's our taxi," said Mr Tate, pointing out a people carrier waiting on the jetty.

"Mum said you can come and stay with us at the B&B for a few nights, Rachel," Kirsty remarked as they left the ferry.

"And you can come and stay at the campsite with us," Rachel added eagerly. "It'll be fun!"

Once the luggage had been packed into the taxi, the driver set off for Mimosa Cottage, the bed and breakfast where the Tates were staying. Rainspell Island was looking especially green and gorgeous, Rachel thought. It was spring and the wildflowers were in full bloom.

Very soon they

arrived at Mimosa Cottage, a pretty little house with a thatched roof.

"Mum, can I go to the campsite with Rachel?" Kirsty asked as the taxi driver unloaded their suitcases.

"Of course," Mrs Tate replied. "We'll come and collect you later."

The campsite was a little further down the road in a large field. Rachel and Kirsty jumped out of the taxi, thrilled to see that Mr and Mrs Walker had hired one of the biggest tents on the site.

"Look, Kirsty, it's just like a canvas house!" Rachel said as she dashed around the tent. "There are separate bedrooms *and* a lounge."

"Brilliant!" laughed Kirsty, just as excited. "We can have a midnight feast without waking up your mum and dad."

"Rachel, why don't you and Kirsty head into town and find out about Crafts Week?" Mrs Walker suggested. "Your dad and I will unpack."

"OK," Rachel agreed.

"There's an information booth in the town square," Mr Walker told the girls. "The organisers will be able to tell you exactly what's happening this week."

The girls left the tent and hurried across the field. The town wasn't very far away at all – in fact, they could see the rooftops in the distance. They climbed over a stile and then

wandered down a twisty country lane.

"I always get the feeling that something magical's going to happen on Rainspell," Kirsty said dreamily.

"That's because it always does!" Rachel laughed.

The girls had been to the town before, so they found their way to the square easily. It was very busy, with lots of families milling

around. In the middle of the square
was a large red-and-white striped tent
with *Rainspell Island Crafts Week*
embroidered on it in gold letters.

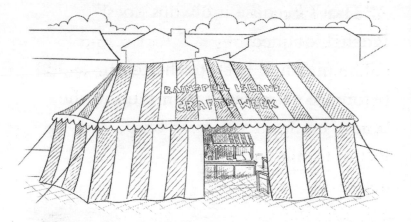

Inside the tent it was even busier.
There was a long line of people queuing
to speak to the organiser, who stood
behind a table piled with leaflets. She
was handing them out as fast as she
could, so the girls joined the end of the
queue to wait patiently for their turn.

"Hello, girls, how can I help you?" the woman asked when Rachel and Kirsty finally reached the table. She was wearing a name badge that said *Artemis Johnson.*

"Hello, Miss Johnson," Kirsty said politely. "My friend Rachel and I would like some information about Crafts Week."

"Do please call me Artie!" The woman beamed at them. "Now, are you interested in any activities in particular?"

"We're staying here for the whole week, so we want to try *everything*," Rachel explained.

"Splendid!" Artie replied. "The crafts activities are taking place all over the island, so here's a map to show you where they are." She handed the map to Kirsty. "There's a pottery class in the hall down by the jetty. You can make jewellery at the accessories shop and learn to bake at the cookie shop, and lots more!"

The girls glanced at each other with delight. They hardly knew where to start!

"Oh, and at the end of the week there'll be a special outdoor exhibition," Artie went on. "Everyone who's taken part in Crafts Week can enter something they've made, and we'll be giving out prizes for the best."

"Thank you, Artie," said Rachel.

"Now before you go, do have a look at our arts and crafts display." Artie gestured at a table on the other side of the tent. "Everything there has been made by our professional Crafts Week instructors."

The girls went over to take a look. The centrepiece of the table was a magnificent strawberry-and-cream cake that made Kirsty's mouth water just by looking at it. The cake was surrounded by paintings of wildflowers and pencil sketches of Rainspell Island, alongside a patchwork quilt, delicate silver jewellery and handmade storybooks with marbled covers. There was also a display of curvy clay pots finished with a vivid blue glaze.

"I'd love to learn how to make a clay pot," Kirsty confided to Rachel.

"I think it's called *throwing* a pot,"
Rachel said with a grin. "Or maybe
that's just what you do if you make
a mistake!"

"Hello, girls," said a tiny voice out of
nowhere. "Would you like to have even
more magical crafts fun?"

Art Attack!

At first Rachel and Kirsty were startled.
Then they both smiled from ear to ear
as they spotted a little fairy peeping over
the rim of one of the shiny blue pots and
waving cheerfully at them.

"I'm Kayla the Pottery Fairy," she
explained, her eyes twinkling merrily.

She looked very pretty in her casual denim shirt dress, cropped dark grey leggings and pink shoes. "I'm one of the seven Magical Crafts Fairies, and I'm here to invite you to a *very* special event in Fairyland, if you'd like to come?"

"Yes please, Kayla," the girls chorused. Even though they'd visited Fairyland many times, it was a still a huge thrill!

Kayla tumbled out of the pot and fluttered underneath the table where she was hidden from view by the folds of the tablecloth.

Rachel and Kirsty quickly followed
her. Then, with one flick of her wand,
Kayla's glittery magic whirled them all
away to Fairyland.

Just a couple of magical seconds later,
the girls found themselves among the
familiar toadstool houses of Fairyland.
They'd arrived in the middle of a huge
crowd of fairies, who were clustered
around a podium that had been set up

on the river bank. Queen Titania and
King Oberon were on the podium,
seated on their golden thrones and
attended by Bertram, their frog footman.
Then Kirsty noticed a silver banner
strung across the top of the podium with
Magical Crafts Week painted on it in
scarlet letters.

Kirsty was amazed. "You're having a Crafts Week, too, Kayla!" she said.

"We certainly are!" Kayla laughed. "It's organised by me and the other Magical Crafts Fairies, so come and meet them. We're just waiting for Queen Titania and King Oberon to declare the Crafts Week open."

Kayla led the way through the crowd towards the podium. The girls followed, waving and calling hello as they spotted lots of their old friends.

At the front of the podium, six fairies were deep in discussion.

"Girls, these are my fellow Magical Crafts Fairies," Kayla said, pointing her wand at each of them in turn. "Annabelle the Drawing Fairy, Zadie the Sewing Fairy, Josie the Jewellery-Making Fairy, Violet the Painting Fairy, Libby the Story-Writing Fairy and Roxie the Baking Fairy."

"Welcome to Magical Crafts Week, girls!" the fairies said, all smiles.

"I'm sure you've guessed already that it's *our* job to make sure that crafts are fun and exciting in both the human and the fairy worlds," Roxie added.

"All the fairies will be trying lots of different crafts, just like you," Kayla told Rachel and Kirsty. "And at the end of the week Queen Titania and King Oberon will pick the best, most beautiful things to decorate their palace."

At that moment Bertram hopped to the front of the podium. "Pray silence for their Royal Majesties, Queen Titania and King Oberon," he proclaimed.

The king and queen stepped forward. "Welcome, one and all, to our Magical Crafts Week," the queen said. "I see that some of our friends have arrived to join us!" And she directed a sweet smile at the girls.

Suddenly, to her surprise, Rachel spotted a green balloon sailing over the heads of the crowd. The balloon was

heading straight towards the podium.
It hit the floor next to Queen Titania
and exploded, splattering bright green
paint all over her sparkling silver gown.
Everyone in the crowd gasped in shock,
and the queen cried out in distress.

"What's happening?" Rachel cried, bewildered. She and Kirsty ducked down as more paint-filled balloons zoomed towards the podium. These balloons burst near the Magical Crafts Fairies, covering *them* in green paint, too.

Each of the Magical Crafts Fairies had been holding a special magical object, and they put them down on the grass as they attempted to clean themselves up. Then Kirsty spotted a familiar, icy figure striding through the crowd.

"We should have guessed, Rachel!"
Kirsty groaned. "Jack Frost!"

Grinning with glee, Jack Frost headed
for the podium. Rachel noticed that he
had a big leather art satchel hanging
from his frosty shoulder. Behind him
scampered a gaggle of goblins, hurling
more paint-filled balloons in every
direction. Some of the fairies ran for
cover while others tried to catch the
balloons before they burst.

Jack Frost jumped up onto the podium. At the same moment the girls heard a shout of dismay from Kayla.

"Jack Frost has stolen all our magical objects!" she cried.

"Of course I have!" Jack Frost sneered triumphantly. Rachel and Kirsty were shocked to see that he was clutching Kayla's vase, along with the other six magical objects. "Don't you know I'm the greatest artist ever? And I'm going to

make sure that no one – fairy or human
– uses these objects to try to be better
than *me*!"

Jack Frost shoved the vase into his
satchel, along with the other magical
objects, as the goblins charged onto the
podium to join him. Then, with one
sweep of his wand, Jack Frost conjured
up a bolt of icy blue magic that whisked
both him and his goblins away to the
human world.

Clay
Catastrophe

"This is a disaster!" King Oberon murmured, shaking his head. "Without the magical objects, crafting everywhere will be ruined. Totally ruined!"

The Magical Crafts Fairies looked around miserably at each other, their wings drooping.

"We can help." Kirsty spoke up from the front of the crowd, "Can't we, Rachel?"

"Of course we can," Rachel agreed. "Jack Frost isn't going to get away with this!"

"Oh, girls, you're always here when we need you," Queen Titania said gratefully. "And the Magical Crafts Fairies will assist you in any way they can."

Kayla wiped a spot of green paint off her nose and beckoned to Rachel and Kirsty. "Let's get back to Rainspell Island right away, girls," she said urgently.

Kayla waved her wand and Rachel and Kirsty felt her powerful magic whisk them up, up and away from Fairyland. There were shouts of *"Good luck!"* from the fairies left behind. Then, just a heartbeat later, the girls found themselves outside the information booth in the town square. Immediately Kayla tucked herself away in Rachel's pocket, out of sight.

"Where shall we start looking for your vase?" Kirsty asked her.

"Jack Frost has probably given the magical objects to his goblins to keep safe," Kayla guessed. "The goblins who have my vase will *definitely* be drawn to doing pottery!"

"Artie said we could try pottery in the hall by the jetty," Rachel reminded

Kirsty. "Let's look there first."

The girls checked the Crafts Week map and then headed to the jetty. On the way Rachel was surprised to see a group of angry people stomp past them, complaining to each other in loud voices about what an awful time they were having. Rachel could see they were spattered with what looked like mud. And they weren't the only ones. More people were trailing along behind them, all stained with mud and all coming from the direction of the jetty.

"I wonder what's going on?" Rachel remarked, puzzled.

At that moment a woman wearing a dirty leather apron came hurrying towards them. Kirsty noticed her name badge – *Madeleine Potts, Pottery Instructor* – and

spoke to her as she
went by.

"Is everything
OK?" Kirsty
asked,
concerned.
"We're just on
our way to your
pottery class."

"I'd advise you
to leave it for a while,
girls," Madeleine Potts replied
in a harassed voice. "Some naughty boys
have been creating havoc, throwing clay
at everyone, including me!" She looked
down at her clay-stained apron. "I'm
going to get Artie to help me sort them
out." Then she dashed off.

"Naughty boys?" Rachel repeated.

"Naughty goblins, I think!"

"Let's go!" Kayla piped up excitedly from Rachel's pocket.

The girls ran the rest of the way to the hall. When they arrived, they could hear shrieks and giggles inside.

"Wait," Kirsty said as Rachel reached for the door handle. "Maybe it would be better if Kayla could turn us into fairies. It'll be easier to stay out of sight."

"You're so right!" Kayla replied with a wink. She shot out of Rachel's pocket, waved her wand and surrounded the girls with a mist of sparkling magic. In a trice, Rachel and Kirsty were the same size as Kayla, with delicate, translucent wings on their backs.

The three of them flew through an open window and, to their horror,

immediately found themselves right in
the middle of a storm of wet clay. Blobs
of it were flying through the air thick
and fast, and Rachel gave a yelp of
surprise as a ball of clay knocked her
off balance, sending her tumbling into
a nosedive. She fought to recover
herself and managed to zoom upwards
again. Meanwhile, Kayla and Kirsty
dodged from side to side, trying to avoid

being hit, too.

Kirsty glanced down and saw two
goblins yelling with glee as they
continued to pelt each other with blob
after blob of clay. Two other goblins
had smeared the floor with more clay
and were enjoying slipping and sliding

around as if they were on a skating rink.
"Madeleine Potts was right," Kirsty

said breathlessly. "It's havoc in here!"

"Let's hide somewhere safe," Kayla suggested. "Then we can plan our next move." She flew down and popped behind a vase that stood in the middle of the potter's wheel. Kirsty and Rachel followed, and as they did so, Kirsty noticed a shelf full of beautiful pots, vases and jars finished with bright, swirling glazes.

"Did the goblins make these?" Kirsty whispered, pointing to the shelf.

"Probably," Kayla replied. "The magic of my vase means they've become master potters!" She frowned. "My vase is somewhere here. I can *feel* it..."

Rachel stared at the shelf, wondering if the goblins had hidden Kayla's vase there with the others. But, just a moment later,

Kayla gave a little squeal of excitement.

"Oh, girls, *look*!" she exclaimed, "Look at that green backpack on the workbench. See the very faint magical haze surrounding it?"

Rachel and Kirsty peered over at the open backpack. Inside it nestled a familiar, sparkly object – Kayla's vase!

"I've got to get it back!" Kayla said in a determined voice. "Wait here, girls." And without delay she whizzed straight towards the backpack. But suddenly a goblin in a clay-smeared apron came out of a cupboard marked *Storeroom*, very close to where the backpack was lying. He was staggering under the weight of a big block of clay. Kirsty and Rachel glanced at each other in dismay.

"Hurry, Kayla!" Kirsty murmured. Their fairy friend still hadn't realised the goblin was close by.

At first the goblin seemed to be heading for the potter's wheel, but to the girls' dismay, he threw a casual glance at his backpack. The goblin scowled ferociously as he spotted Kayla just about to dart inside it. He dropped the block of clay on the workbench and lunged at the little fairy.

"Kayla, look out!" Kirsty shouted.

In a Spin!

Kayla tried to flee, but she was too late. The goblin captured her in his clay-stained hands and held her tightly.

"Let me go!" Kayla demanded. "I just want my magical vase back."

"Well, you're not having it!" the goblin retorted rudely. "I *love* pottery. See all these beautiful things I made?" He pointed proudly at the shelf. "Well, no fairy's going to spoil *my* fun!"

Rachel and Kirsty watched from
the potter's wheel as the goblin lifted
the lid off one of the jars on the shelf.
He dropped Kayla inside and replaced
the lid firmly.

"Kayla's trapped!" Rachel said. "We
must rescue her, Kirsty."

But before the girls had had time to
think up a plan, the goblin came over
to the potter's wheel and sat down to
examine the vase he'd made earlier.

"This vase needs a little more work," he muttered to himself. He sat down on the stool and then pressed his big green foot down hard on the operating pedal. The wheel immediately began to whirl round and round, taking Rachel and Kirsty with it.

"Hold on, Kirsty!" Rachel gasped, clutching the edge of the wheel tightly. Kirsty did the same as the wheel gathered speed.

After a moment or two, the girls were spinning around so fast that the room became a blur, and they began to feel

sick and dizzy. Very soon they could
hold on no longer.
Both Rachel and
Kirsty were thrown
off the whirring
wheel, up
into the air.
They tumbled
down into the
vase the goblin
was making and
landed on the damp clay
at the bottom. The girls lay there, feeling
more than a little dazed.

The goblin hadn't noticed them and
luckily, just a few seconds later, he
brought the wheel to a stop.

"Thank goodness!" Rachel murmured.
"I'm so dizzy, I'm seeing double!"

"This clay is really wet and sticky," Kirsty complained, flicking a blob of it off one of her wings. Then Rachel saw her friend's eyes light up. "Oh!"  Kirsty exclaimed. "That's just given me an idea!"

Quickly Kirsty whispered her plan to Rachel. Then, together, the two girls popped up out of the vase, just as Kayla had done when they first met her. The goblin stared at them in disbelief, and then let out a shriek of rage.

"More fairies!" he roared. "I *hate* fairies! They're annoying, interfering, nosy little busybodies!"

"We just wanted to say how much we love your vase," Kirsty said with a smile.

The goblin looked shocked. Then he grinned proudly.

"In fact, if your vase was a bit taller, I'm sure you'd win one of the Crafts Week prizes," Rachel told him.

"Yes, I think I would too, because I'm *obviously* the best potter on the whole of Rainspell Island!" the goblin boasted.

"If you stood on your stool, you'd be able to reach the top of the vase to make it taller," Kirsty pointed out innocently.

"You know, that's not a bad idea for a silly little fairy!" the goblin said. He hopped up onto the stool, stood on tiptoe and leaned over the vase. Silently Kirsty beckoned to Rachel and they flew behind him.

"Here we go, Rachel," Kirsty whispered. "After three!"

Precious Pot

"One – two – THREE!" said Kirsty. And on the count of three, the girls zoomed towards the goblin and gave him a push.

"Stop that!" the goblin yelled furiously, teetering back and forth on his stool. He lost his balance and then fell headfirst into the clay vase in front of him. The only things the girls could see were his big green feet sticking out of the top.

"Help!" came a muffled voice from inside the vase. Kirsty glanced over at the other goblins. They were still too busy playing with the clay and hadn't noticed a thing so far.

"Now to rescue Kayla!" Rachel said breathlessly, and she and Kirsty flew at top speed over to the shelf.

"Which pot is she in?" asked Kirsty. But then they heard a tiny voice calling to them.

"Girls, girls, I'm inside the blue jar with the red lid!"

Together Rachel and Kirsty found the jar and struggled to lift up the heavy lid. They just managed to raise it enough for Kayla to fly out of the gap. The little fairy looked very relieved and gave them both a grateful hug.

"I see you managed to deal with the goblin!" Kayla whispered with a grin as she spotted his feet waving around in the air. "Well done, girls. Now I can retrieve my beautiful vase!"

Kayla swooped down towards the backpack. With one quick movement, she scooped up her vase, and instantly it shrank to its fairy size, shimmering with a wonderful, magical glow.

Kayla tucked the vase safely under her arm before heading back to Rachel and Kirsty.

"Let's get out of here, girls," she began. But suddenly the goblin inside the pot summoned up all his breath and roared "HELP!" at the very top of his lungs.

This time the other goblins heard him. They turned around, saw his feet sticking out of the vase and dashed towards him. But the floor was wet and sticky with all the clay they'd been throwing around, and the goblins began slipping and sliding all over the place. With shouts and squeals, they crashed into the potter's wheel, knocking the vase to the floor. The result was a heap of goblins floundering around in a big pile of mucky wet clay, with the goblin potter right in the middle.

"Oh dear, what a terrible mess!" Kayla sighed.

One of the goblins looked up. "That pesky fairy has her magic vase back!" he pointed out, wiping a smear of clay off his nose. All the goblins looked very disappointed, but especially the one who had made the beautiful pots on the shelf.

The goblins hauled themselves to their feet and then, with many loud moans and groans about how cross Jack Frost was going to be, they trudged gloomily over to the door. The goblin potter hung back, taking a long, sad look at the pots he'd made.

Rachel and Kirsty exchanged a glance. Then together they fluttered over to the shelf and picked up a small but very pretty green pot, the only one they could lift between them. Quickly they flew over to the goblin and presented him with the pot.

"Oh!" The goblin couldn't believe his eyes. "Thank you!" And he skipped out of the hall, holding the pot as carefully as if it were precious treasure.

"Girls, you're very
kind," Kayla said
with a smile.
"You've made
a goblin
and a fairy
extremely
happy today
– thank you,
thank you, a
thousand times!
I can't wait to get back to Fairyland
with the fantastic news. But first I have a
little more work to do here..."

One flick of Kayla's wand restored
Rachel and Kirsty to their human size.
Then a second burst of magical fairy
sparkles cleaned up the hall in the
twinkling of an eye.

"Someone's coming, girls," Kayla whispered as they heard voices outside the hall. "I must go. But I know you'll be on the lookout for more of our magical objects!"

"We will, Kayla," Rachel cried. "Goodbye!"

"Goodbye," Kirsty echoed, as Kayla vanished in a cloud of sparkly fairy dust.

Glittering Glazes

At that moment Madeleine Potts walked in with Artie. They both looked surprised but pleased to find the hall empty except for the girls.

"Those naughty boys must have gone," Artie said, looking around. "You can carry on with your class, Madeleine."

"Thank you for cleaning up, girls," Madeleine said gratefully as Artie left the hall. "Would you like to try your hand at making pots?"

"We'd love to!" Rachel replied.

Madeleine showed the girls how to knead, cut and layer the clay to make it soft to work with. Then Kirsty began to roll lengths of clay to make a coil pot, while Madeleine taught Rachel how to use the potter's wheel.

"You're learning very quickly, Rachel," Madeleine said approvingly, watching as Rachel carefully moulded a small pot on the spinning wheel. Rachel smiled, but didn't say that this wasn't her first experience with the potter's wheel that day!

More people wandered into the hall, as

the girls were preparing different-colour glazes to add to their pots once they had been fired. Soon the whole place was buzzing with laughter and conversation, as Madeleine was kept busy helping everyone with their clay creations.

"I'll fire your pots in the kiln now, girls," she told Rachel and Kirsty. "Come back this afternoon, and they'll be ready for you. I'll add the glazes you've prepared."

"I can't wait to see them!" Rachel said to Kirsty as they went back to the

campsite for lunch.

Later that day the girls rushed back to the hall to collect their clay pots. They were both fizzing with excitement. The last few people were finishing off their pots with Madeleine's help, but when she saw Rachel and Kirsty, she hurried over to them.

"I think you're going to be very pleased, girls!" Madeleine said, ushering

them over to a table crammed with pots.
At the front was Kirsty's coil pot, with
a pink and purple glaze that sparkled
just like Kayla's vase. Next to it was
Rachel's hand-thrown pot, glazed in red
and green and glittering just as brightly.

"I don't know how you two managed
to get your glazes to sparkle like that,"
Madeleine said admiringly, "but they
look wonderful!"

Kirsty and Rachel exchanged a
quick, secret smile. They knew it was

fairy magic!

And, although they'd already found Kayla's vase, the girls knew that this was only the beginning of their Crafts Week adventures. Six magical objects were still missing, and it was up to Rachel and Kirsty – and their friends the Magical Crafts Fairies – to bring them home to Fairyland!

The End

Now it's time for Kirsty and
Rachel to help…

Annabelle the Drawing Fairy

Read on for a sneak peek…

"I think that Rainspell Island is my favourite place in the whole world!" said Kirsty Tate, twirling on the spot.

Her best friend Rachel Walker jumped up and took Kirsty's hands. They spun around in a circle until they fell down on the grass, dizzy and happy. It was springtime, and the campsite meadow was full of daisies and buttercups.

"The sun always shines on Rainspell Island," Rachel said, laughing.

Rainspell Island was the place where Rachel and Kirsty first became friends, and where they first began their adventures with the fairies. Now they were back there again with their families for Crafts Week.

Every day, the girls could take different classes in all sorts of arts and crafts, from painting to making jewellery. On the final day there was going to be an exhibition and competition, with prizes!

Read **Annabelle the Drawing Fairy** to find out what adventures are in store for Kirsty and Rachel!

Join in the magic online by signing up to the Rainbow Magic fan club!

Sign up today at:
www.rainbowmagicbooks.co.uk

Meet the
Magical Crafts Fairies

Jack Frost has stolen the Magical Crafts Fairies' special objects. Can Kirsty and Rachel help get them back before Rainspell Island's Crafts Week is ruined?

www.rainbowmagicbooks.co.uk

Competition!

The Magical Crafts Fairies have created a special
competition just for you!
In the back of each book in the Magical Crafts series there
will be a question for you to answer.
First you need to collect the answer from the back
of each book in the series.
Once you have all the answers, take the first letter from
each one and arrange them to spell a secret word!
When you have the answer, go online and enter!

**In Kayla the Pottery Fairy, where
do Kirsty and Rachel go for
Crafts Week?**

_ _ _ _ _ _ _ _

_ _ _ _ _

We will put all the correct entries into a draw and select
a winner to receive a special Rainbow Magic Goody Bag
featuring lots of treats for you and your fairy friends.
You'll also star in a new Rainbow Magic story!

Enter online now at www.rainbowmagicbooks.co.uk

Have you read them all?

The Rainbow Fairies

1. Ruby the Red Fairy ☑
2. Amber the Orange Fairy ☑
3. Saffron the Yellow Fairy ☑
4. Fern the Green Fairy ☐
5. Sky the Blue Fairy ☐
6. Izzy the Indigo Fairy ☑
7. Heather the Violet Fairy ☑

The Weather Fairies

8. Crystal the Snow Fairy ☐
9. Abigail the Breeze Fairy ☐
10. Pearl the Cloud Fairy ☐
11. Goldie the Sunshine Fairy ☐
12. Evie the Mist Fairy ☐
13. Storm the Lightning Fairy ☐
14. Hayley the Rain Fairy ☐

The Party Fairies

15. Cherry the Cake Fairy ☐
16. Melodie the Music Fairy ☐
17. Grace the Glitter Fairy ☐
18. Honey the Sweet Fairy ☐
19. Polly the Party Fun Fairy ☐
20. Phoebe the Fashion Fairy ☐
21. Jasmine the Present Fairy ☐

The Jewel Fairies

22. India the Moonstone Fairy ☐
23. Scarlett the Garnet Fairy ☐
24. Emily the Emerald Fairy ☐
25. Chloe the Topaz Fairy ☐
26. Amy the Amethyst Fairy ☐
27. Sophie the Sapphire Fairy ☐
28. Lucy the Diamond Fairy ☐

The Pet Keeper Fairies

29. Katie the Kitten Fairy ☐
30. Bella the Bunny Fairy ☐
31. Georgia the Guinea Pig Fairy ☐
32. Lauren the Puppy Fairy ☐
33. Harriet the Hamster Fairy ☐
34. Molly the Goldfish Fairy ☑
35. Penny the Pony Fairy ☐

The Fun Day Fairies

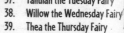
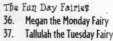
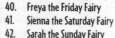

36. Megan the Monday Fairy
37. Tallulah the Tuesday Fairy
38. Willow the Wednesday Fairy
39. Thea the Thursday Fairy
40. Freya the Friday Fairy
41. Sienna the Saturday Fairy
42. Sarah the Sunday Fairy

The Petal Fairies

43. Tia the Tulip Fairy
44. Pippa the Poppy Fairy
45. Louise the Lily Fairy
46. Charlotte the Sunflower Fairy
47. Olivia the Orchid Fairy
48. Danielle the Daisy Fairy
49. Ella the Rose Fairy

The Dance Fairies

50. Bethany the Ballet Fairy
51. Jade the Disco Fairy
52. Rebecca the Rock'n'Roll Fairy
53. Tasha the Tap Dance Fairy
54. Jessica the Jazz Fairy
55. Saskia the Salsa Fairy
56. Imogen the Ice Dance Fairy

The Sporty Fairies

57. Helena the Horseriding Fairy
58. Francesca the Football Fairy
59. Zoe the Skating Fairy
60. Naomi the Netball Fairy
61. Samantha the Swimming Fairy
62. Alice the Tennis Fairy
63. Gemma the Gymnastics Fairy

The Music Fairies

64. Poppy the Piano Fairy
65. Ellie the Guitar Fairy
66. Fiona the Flute Fairy
67. Danni the Drum Fairy
68. Maya the Harp Fairy
69. Victoria the Violin Fairy
70. Sadie the Saxophone Fairy

The Magical Animal Fairies

71. Ashley the Dragon Fairy ☐
72. Lara the Black Cat Fairy ☐
73. Erin the Firebird Fairy ☐
74. Rihanna the Seahorse Fairy ☐
75. Sophia the Snow Swan Fairy ☐
76. Leona the Unicorn Fairy ☐
77. Caitlin the Ice Bear Fairy ☐

The Green Fairies

78. Nicole the Beach Fairy ☐
79. Isabella the Air Fairy ☐
80. Edie the Garden Fairy ☐
81. Coral the Reef Fairy ☐
82. Lily the Rainforest Fairy ☐
83. Carrie the Snow Cap Fairy ☐
84. Milly the River Fairy ☐

The Ocean Fairies

85. Ally the Dolphin Fairy ☐
86. Amelie the Seal Fairy ☐
87. Pia the Penguin Fairy ☐
88. Tess the Sea Turtle Fairy ☐
89. Stephanie the Starfish Fairy ☐
90. Whitney the Whale Fairy ☐
91. Courtney the Clownfish Fairy ☐

The Twilight Fairies

92. Ava the Sunset Fairy ☐
93. Lexi the Firefly Fairy ☐
94. Zara the Starlight Fairy ☐
95. Morgan the Midnight Fairy ☐
96. Yasmin the Night Owl Fairy ☐
97. Maisie the Moonbeam Fairy ☐
98. Sabrina the Sweet Dreams Fairy ☐

The Showtime Fairies

99. Madison the Magic Show Fairy ☐
100. Leah the Theatre Fairy ☐
101. Alesha the Acrobat Fairy ☐
102. Darcey the Dance Diva Fairy ☐
103. Taylor the Talent Show Fairy ☐
104. Amelia the Singing Fairy ☐
105. Isla the Ice Star Fairy ☐

The Princess Fairies

106. Honor the Happy Days Fairy ☐
107. Demi the Dressing-Up Fairy ☐
108. Anya the Cuddly Creatures Fairy ☐
109. Elisa the Adventure Fairy ☐
110. Lizzie the Sweet Treats Fairy ☐
111. Maddie the Playtime Fairy ☐
112. Eva the Enchanted Ball Fairy ☐

The Pop Star Fairies

113. Jessie the Lyrics Fairy ☐
114. Adele the Singing Coach Fairy ☐
115. Vanessa the Dance Steps Fairy ☐
116. Miley the Stylist Fairy ☐
117. Frankie the Make-Up Fairy ☐
118. Rochelle the Star Spotter Fairy ☐
119. Una the Concert Fairy ☐

The Fashion Fairies

120. Miranda the Beauty Fairy ☐
121. Claudia the Accessories Fairy ☐
12.2. Tyra the Dress Designer Fairy ☐
123. Alexa the Fashion Reporter Fairy ☐
124. Matilda the Hair Stylist Fairy ☐
125. Brooke the Photographer Fairy ☐
126. Lola the Fashion Fairy ☐

The Sweet Fairies

127. Lottie the Lollipop Fairy ☐
128. Esme the Ice Cream Fairy ☐
129. Coco the Cupcake Fairy ☐
130. Clara the Chocolate Fairy ☐
131. Madeleine the Cookie Fairy ☐
132. Layla the Candyfloss Fairy ☐
133. Nina the Birthday Cake Fairy ☐

The Baby Animal Rescue Fairies

134. Mae the Panda Fairy ☐
135. Kitty the Tiger Fairy ☐
136. Mara the Meerkat Fairy ☐
137. Savannah the Zebra Fairy ☐
138. Kimberley the Koala Fairy ☐
139. Rosie the Honey Bear Fairy ☐
140. Anna the Arctic Fox Fairy ☐

The Magical Crafts Fairies

141. Kayla the Pottery Fairy ☐
142. Annabelle the Drawing Fairy ☐
143. Zadie the Sewing Fairy ☐
144. Josie the Jewellery-Making Fairy ☐
145. Violet the Painting Fairy ☐
146. Libby the Story-Writing Fairy ☐
147. Roxie the Baking Fairy ☐

There's a book of fairy fun for everyone!

www.rainbowmagicbooks.co.uk

Lila & Myla
the Twins
Fairies

Meet Lila and Myla the Twins Fairies!
Can the fairies stop Jack Frost before he uses
their magic to create his very own twin?

www.rainbowmagicbooks.co.uk